IT WATCHES
ANGELA DUNHAM

For more information, please email angiedunham@gmail.com

CONTENTS

PROLOGUE

L IGHT. SOUND. IT DIDN'T understand why it had words for these things, but they existed, just like it did. It hadn't been here moments ago, but now it was. Something had brought it into existence with a bang, tethering it to the earth. Stretching out in its bodily form, it felt strong. Chanting sounds drifted from somewhere in the distance. Turning, it saw a picture take shape on the other side of the floating square. Staring out through what it called eyes, four figures came into focus. Moving closer to the sound, it noticed the four-sided box created a barrier between it and what it wanted.

Reaching up with hands, yes, the two spindly appendages on the ends of its arms were called hands; it pressed them against the hard, transparent substance. Glass, the word rang out inside its mind. The floating square was just a piece of glass, and four young girls sat in a circle on the other side, surrounded by a ring made of white powder. The one with the red hair felt familiar and was reading aloud from an old, worn brown book. The girls were casting a spell. A feeling of dread washed over it, and it banged its fists against the glass in outrage. None of the girls noticed. It didn't understand why it wanted to hurt them, but the urge was all-consuming. It was trapped, and this place behind the glass was a cage—a cage built by the ones on the outside. It chose a random direction and began walking, only to be returned to the exact center point behind the glass. It repeated the action, over and over, until it tired of the game. Its prison was an inky velvet box. There was only darkness and the glass. It would find a way out, and when it did, they would all pay.

CHAPTER I

S ARIN DELVAUX STRETCHED OUT in her cozy bed. It was still dark out, but her annoying alarm clock said it was time to wake up. Groaning, she rolled over and slammed her hand over the snooze button for the fifth time. The chalky taste in her mouth reminded her of the spell-casting nightmare that had gone down the night before. Sarin should have been well versed in all aspects of magic at age twenty, but her non-magical mother couldn't teach her, and her witch of a father wasn't in the picture. In these non-magical times, the coven elders frowned upon even the most basic forms of witchcraft. Thousands of people still visited metaphysical shops, read books on paganism, and claimed to study the moon's cycles, but not many possessed raw magic.

The real Wiccans' had all been forced into hiding or chosen to give up their magic to survive. Blending in was vital to preventing a revival of the witch trials, so Sarin paid her dues. Sarin knew nothing about her magical heritage, but her mother claimed she was a spirit witch. Precisely what that entailed was still murky at best. She had visions that rarely came to fruition, and her mind-reading skills were spotty on a good day. If she was being honest with herself, she felt more like a Pisces in crisis during PMS week than an actual witch. Her dad had passed away in a tragic fire before she'd been born, and with no other family left on his side, there was no one left to help her navigate these magical problems. The only connection to the magical world she had was her best friend, Faith Bradbury, whose gem of a soul had walked into her life two years ago when she'd applied to the Nursing Program at Georgian College. The small town of Huntsville, Ontario, was a hard place to make friends, let alone a witchy one like herself, so their meeting had felt like fate. Faith's family had relocated to the area a few years ago after her mother claimed the land inside the Algonquin Provincial Park held a spark of magic that called to her. Sarin had grown up playing in those woods and had never felt anything but the awe of the great outdoors. But who was she to judge what other witches claimed to be true? Faith and her younger cousins were left to fend for themselves most weekends while their parents gallivanted around the park searching for some magical beacon. Faith's mother wasn't a sharer, so Faith had yet to learn what they were genuinely looking for. That wasn't surprising since most witches tended to be paranoid. Faith's mother, Farrow, and the twins' mother, Fallon, were no exception. They also forbid the younger generation from practicing magic, especially her. Faith said her Delvaux surname scared Farrow, but Sarin didn't understand why. As far as she knew, she was the last Delvaux witch in existence, the rest having perished in the same fire that claimed her father's life.

Staring up at the ceiling, Sarin cursed. She would be late for class if she didn't get up now. Grabbing the glass on her nightstand, she downed what was left of her water to try and wash away the magical residue that clung to her tongue like a winter coat. Magical hangovers were far worse than alcohol-induced ones. Last night, she and Faith had attempted a simple glamour spell. Well, simple in theory. In reality, the poor little tree frog they'd tried to glamour to look like a butterfly had gone crazy, grown twenty times in size, and chased them around the room for half an hour before clawing Sarin's cheek with its sharp talons. At that point, Sarin had taken matters into her own hands and hit the frog over the head with a book to knock it out. The magical backlash from causing harm to the innocent creature packed a mean punch that left her dry-heaving for three hours while Faith broke out in warts. The golden rule was to do no harm, but what was she supposed to do when a mutant ninja frog attempted to claw her face off? The tiny amphibian was no worse for wear, but from now on, they'd be using inanimate objects for all magical testing until they got the hang of casting.

Rushing to make herself somewhat presentable, Sarin sprinted around her small but tidy bedroom, grabbing any random clothes she could find and praying they were clean. The house she shared with her mother was a cozy two-story bungalow with a big wrap-around front porch. In the spring, Sarin loved to sit outside and enjoy the view of the creek that ran down the side of the property. She loved everything about the house, except for the detached garage- because, in winter, you had to trudge through the snow to get to your car. It was an annoying, freezing pain in the ass. Pausing on the second-floor landing, she took a moment to inspect her wrinkled mess of a self in the tall floor-length mirror. She looked exactly how she felt, like one enormous pile of shit. Stepping into the hallway bathroom, she pulled her messy mop of red hair into a bun and vigorously brushed her teeth to try to remove the last remnants of magical grime stuck to her teeth. When the gross flavor refused to vacate her mouth, she threw the toothbrush into the trash and ran downstairs, hoping she would make it to class on time.

CHAPTER 2

S ARIN WAS GRATEFUL FOR the silence the classroom afforded her. The only person she even remotely cared about talking to was Faith, and that girl was currently passed out on her desk, face down. In retrospect, breaking out in warts for hours and not knowing if they would ever go away would keep anyone up all night. Sarin let out an audible sigh as she thumbed through her note cards from last week's lecture. Her ultimate dream was to heal people by whatever magical or non-magical means she could harness. After graduation, she could use real-world knowledge to make a difference in people's health, even if the magical route didn't pan out.

"Mrs. Bradbury!" Mr. Henley called out in an annoyed voice.

Glancing up from her notes, Sarin saw that Faith was still sleeping. Shit, she thought, there was no helping her friend get out of this one.

"Mrs. Bradbury!" Mr. Henley called again, louder this time.

Faith's messy blonde head snapped up in surprise.

"Would you care to fail my class?"

Faith's face flushed a bright shade of red as she fumbled with her words, "Um, I'm so sorry, Mr. H. To be honest, I don't feel very well."

"Then maybe you should take the day off instead of sleeping in my class."

Nodding, Faith quickly packed up her messenger bag and bolted out of the classroom.

"Now, where were we?" Mr. H continued, "Sarin, can you tell me what suffix most beta-blockers have?"

Year two of the nursing program was far more challenging than the first year. Sprinkle in the required nursing placements and a shit storm of magical mayhem, and that equaled a lot of sleepless nights. Scouring her exhausted, slow-thinking brain for the answer, Sarin silently cursed Mr. H for being so hard on Faith.

Unsure of the correct response, she took a guess. "Um? Is it Olol?"

"That's correct. Glad to see someone is paying attention today."

Sarin lowered her eyes at his backhanded compliment. She wanted to be in this program, but the more she practiced magic, the less she focused on the non-magical world. Wrangling both sides of herself was tricky, but

Sarin knew if she gave up on magic, she'd destroy a small piece of her soul and the only piece of her father she possessed. The only realistic solution was to learn how to control her powers and find a way to integrate them into her everyday life. And to achieve that goal, she needed to convince Faith's mother to teach her how to use magic properly, whether the stuck-up bitch wanted to or not. Sarin had every right to know about her magical heritage, and if Farrow Bradbury was hiding information about her family, then it was high time the witch came clean. Sarin hadn't pushed the issue sooner because she adored Faith and didn't want to jeopardize their friendship, but they were at a stalemate. It was time to have an uncomfortable conversation with Faith about confronting her mother. Fidgeting in her seat, Sarin hoped Faith would be open to the conversation, or she might be left to deal with magically deranged frogs for the rest of her life.

CHAPTER 3

A FTER CLASS, SARIN RUSHED through the parking to get to her mom's worn-down Nissan Rogue. Digging her cell phone from her messenger bag, she immediately called Faith.

"I don't want to talk about it!" Faith declared in a defeated voice on the other end of the line.

Putting a pin in the mom harassment train, Sarin shifted gears to comfort her friend. "Why are you sweating it? And since when do you care about what those tools in our class think?"

Ignoring the question, Faith let out an audible huff. "I need a drink. Can you meet me at Mills in thirty?"

Mills was one of the few good bars on Main Street and a popular hangout for all the college kids. With its extensive beer list and majestic river views, Sarin never passed up a chance to drink there.

"Yeah, I can head over now and catch you up on our lecture notes."

"Thanks, Sarin, I owe you one."

Placing her cell phone in the center console, Sarin hoped she could use the favor to her advantage and score an invite to dinner.

Downtown Huntsville was only five minutes from campus, so Sarin knew she'd be early. Parking directly in front of Mills, she took a short walk on the trail behind Main Street to enjoy the awe-inspiring view of the Muskoka Rivera. Water always comforted her, and the river's gentle flowing waves, set against the lush blanket of green trees, brought her frantic thoughts back into focus. When the world was quiet, her intuition spoke the loudest; in this peaceful place, it screamed that something big was coming. That knowing feeling she'd always had deep in her gut told her the first step was to learn to harness her power. The rest would come later. Taking a deep, centering breath, Sarin didn't even blink when Faith snuck up behind her. As a spirit witch, she could feel other people's auras, but she gave Faith a solid A for effort.

"Not even close," Sarin called out over her shoulder.

"Damn it! I'm going to get you one day. Just wait."

"It's good to have goals," Sarin quipped, "but my ESP is on point."

Smiling, Faith locked her arms around Sarin's.

Gesturing toward the historic Swing Bridge, Faith asked, "I wonder how many people have jumped?"

"Morbid much?" Sarin joked.

Faith was a little too obsessed with death, always plotting out the worst-case scenario.

"I'm just saying. The bridge isn't high enough to kill you if you fell, but with the freezing waters in the winter, you'd get hypothermia almost immediately. Not the worst way to go."

Sarin's lips curled into a smirk. "And what would be the best way?"

Shrugging, Faith squeezed her arm a little tighter. "I'll get back to you after we finish our nurse training."

Amused by her answer, Sarin pulled her friend toward the back door entrance of Mills, and as they walked through the double doors, Sarin smelled the thick aroma of lavender and stale beer. The bar owner moonlighted as a Reiki healer and always had a burning diffuser of essential oils. It was a strange scent combination but not horrible. It was still early afternoon, so the bar was quiet. Heading toward their usual table in the back corner, Sarin cringed when she noticed who was working behind the bar. Hazel-colored eyes tracked her as she walked in. Alex Blackstone worked part-time bartending while he and his brother cultivated their fledgling media company. Blackstone & Blackstone had just celebrated its first anniversary, but it seemed like Alex still wasn't ready to pivot into full adulthood. Alex wasn't ready for a lot of things. Sarin knew from firsthand experience.

"Hey, Karin!" he called out, his voice smooth as silk.

She hated that nickname. You yell at one neighbor for turning the sprinklers on a first grader running around in her yard, and you're forever the Karin.

Turning to face her ex, Sarin couldn't help but flush. Somehow, Alex only got better looking with time. It wasn't fair. Their relationship had been intense but short-lived, and after she caught him cheating six months ago, she'd jumped ship and never looked back. Cyber-stalking aside.

Rolling her eyes, Sarin ignored his prodding. "What ciders do you have on draft this month?"

Smiling, Alex handed her a menu from across the bar. "A few. Take a look."

"You do work here, right? You're standing behind the bar, wearing all black, which is the standard uniform. Or are the clothes just some new Goth look you're trying? No? You're an employee, so please tell me what's on draft?"

"If I made it easy for you, then I wouldn't get to participate in all this super fun banter, now, would I?"

The prick winked at her. Blood boiling, Sarin snatched the menu from him before dragging a wide-eyed Faith toward a table in the back.

"You're doing it again," Faith said as they sat down.

Grumbling over the menu, Sarin asked, "Doing what, exactly?"

"Letting that asshole get under your skin."

"I'm not letting him do anything!" Sarin stated as she slammed the menu down on the table. "Why did you want to come here, anyway?"

"He's usually off on Thursdays. You know this."

Faith was right. Sarin was letting her temper get the best of her, something she knew she should not do. Not when you had an uncontrolled magical arsenal writhing underneath your skin. Taking a deep, calming breath, Sarin counted to five in her head.

"You're right. I'm sorry. God, he just makes me so angry."

Faith reached across the table and patted her hand. "It will get easier."

"I hope you're right, but can you do me a solid for today and order our drinks? I don't want to talk to him again."

"Of course. What do you want?"

Scanning the menu, Sarin picked a dry pineapple cider, and when Faith came back, she raised a glass to her friend before getting into the nitty gritty of why she had agreed to this meeting in the first place.

"Are you feeling any better since leaving class?" Sarin asked causally.

Faith pushed her dark hair over one shoulder as she sipped on her beer. "I guess. The entire thing was just so embarrassing."

"We need to get a handle on our magic-wielding before something worse happens," Sarin whispered.

"Agreed," Faith said, holding her glass up for another clink.

This was Sarin's opportunity. "Why do you think your mom doesn't want to train us?"

Faith shrugged. "Aside from the obvious need to stay under the radar, I have no idea."

"I know she doesn't like talking about magic or her coven, but I need to know more, and she's the only person with answers. Can I come over and try to talk to her?" Sarin pleaded.

"I don't know, Sarin. My aunt won't train the twins either, and they're adamant about keeping a low profile."

"Don't you want to know why?" Sarin questioned.

"It's the exposure thing. Less chance of people finding out what we are if we don't use our powers."

"That's not fair. Magic is a fundamental part of who we are, and look at what happened last night. What if we make something worse happen because we're inexperienced? What happens if we get angry or sad and our powers explode? You know our powers are tied to our emotions, even if we aren't actively practicing. I want to learn for many reasons, but one of the main ones is so we don't accidentally expose ourselves."

"I'm with you, Sarin, but aside from stealing her grimoire, I don't know what else to do."

"Invite me over for dinner, and let me talk to her. Then, if nothing else, I'll be your accomplice in stealing the book."

Smiling despite the scared look in her eyes, Faith finally conceded. "Okay, but it's your funeral."

CHAPTER 4

Sarin paced around her bedroom, nervous about the big dinner at Faith's house. Everyone, including Faith's aunt Fallon and her twin cousins, would be there. Sarin felt mildly prepared to face Farrow, but now, with Fallon in tow, it would be two against one. Fallon's twin daughters, Phoebe and Selene, were about to turn seventeen and still hadn't come into their magical elements. The twins could boost the potency of a spell in a group setting but couldn't access or wield magic on their own. Sarin liked to think of them as magical amplifiers. Sarin didn't know how to access all of her magic either, but she'd always been in touch with certain parts of her power, yet the twins had no hints of magic, not even a spark inside themselves individually. It was another sad example of why Fallon and

Farrow needed to get off their high horses and teach them. They had four potential witch bombs running around in the community untethered.

Grabbing her mother's car keys off the kitchen countertop, Sarin reminded herself to put a leash on her anger. If Fallon dismissed her because she came in hot, then she'd be Shit out of luck. Her cell phone pinged just as she was about to walk out the door. Pulling it out of her purse to ensure it wasn't' Faith trying to cancel, her heart fluttered when she read who it was from.

Alex: I'm seriously offended you didn't say goodbye to me yesterday.

Rolling her eyes, Sarin shoved her phone into the back pocket of her jeans. There was no point in engaging with him. Nothing good could come of it except for a great night of sex she would immediately regret. They hadn't spoken since their breakup, so why was he contacting her now? Maybe his flavor of the week was busy. Or maybe he was trying to get under her skin. Pissed at herself for giving him any of her headspace, she cursed when she realized she was running late.

Pulling up in front of Faith's house, Sarin put the car in park and froze as a wave of anxiety washed over her. Leaning her head against the headrest, she wished she knew a spell to tamp down her fear or one to make Farrow spill all her secrets without prompting. Settling for a Tums to calm her nervous stomach, she finally mustered up the courage to walk to the front door. Phoebe answered after the first knock, practically tackling her with a hug. Selene was next in line, raising her hand for a fist bump instead of a hug. The twins looked similar with their raven-tinted hair and stormy gray-colored eyes, but that's where the similarities ended. They had completely different personalities. Phoebe was easygoing and affectionate, while Selene was cunning and quiet.

"I'm glad to see you both," Sarin said warmly.

"We heard about the frog." Phoebe giggled. "Maybe next time you should ask us to help."

"At least the frog lived. Who knows what you two menaces would have done to that helpless amphibian?"

Selene snorted. "I would have sold it on the black market. Do you know how much cash you could've made?"

Sarin knew Selene wasn't joking, and that truth was somewhat terrifying. "You know this is why your magic is delayed, right? The universe knows you'll only use them for evil."

"You say evil; I say opportunity," Selene quipped.

Faith chose that moment to save her from the twin tornadoes. "Are you ready for the inquisition?"

"Is that what we're calling it?"

"Do the words probe, shake-down, or debriefing sound better?"

"How about we just eat dinner and see what happens?"

The twins snickered to each other as Sarin followed them into the kitchen, where Farrow and Fallon were busy transferring all the food into serving dishes.

Farrow stopped to hug Sarin, but the embrace was devoid of warmth. "So glad you could join us tonight."

"Thank you for having me. I always love eating your food."

That wasn't a lie. Farrow was a force of nature in the kitchen.

"That's sweet of you to say. Why don't you girls help me carry the rest of this to the table, and then we can dig in?"

"It's good to see you, Sarin," Fallon offered as she uncorked a bottle of red wine. Her words were nice, but Fallon's piercing blue stare said she felt differently.

An hour later, Sarin's stomach was full of the best-roasted chicken she'd ever had, and if she was being honest with herself, she felt content. Or that was the wine talking. The night was going so well that she almost regretted what was coming. Then, true to fashion, Farrow had to go and open her big, fat mouth.

"Faith told us about the spell-casting incident that went south. We warned you girls about the dangers of playing with magic unsupervised. What is it going to take for you to listen? What if that frog had escaped?"

Sarin was so tired of this same old song and dance. Downing her second glass of wine, she finally let her thoughts fly free. "Why are you so sure abstinence is the best policy? If you trained us, things like that wouldn't happen. Magic is in our blood and won't disappear just because you wish it. Leaving us in the dark is only making things worse."

Farrow slammed her cup down on the table. "You have no idea what you're talking about. We've only survived this long because we don't practice openly."

Sarin rolled her eyes. "Then, what are you doing in the forest every weekend, searching for elk? Please, I'm not that stupid. I've read about the magical vortex that is supposed to exist in those woods. Why would you be looking for it if you're not practicing? And I'm not asking to practice openly. I'm asking you to teach me behind closed doors."

"You're speaking on things you know nothing about," Farrow spat.

Sarin was over the cryptic bullshit.

Chancing a glance at Faith, her friend nodded in approval, and that was all the ammunition Sarin needed to push harder.

"See, that's the problem. If you told us the truth, then I wouldn't be talking out of my ass. Why don't we try a different question? Did you know my father? Or anyone on his side of my family?"

"No, I don't."

Sarin could practically taste the lie. "Then, why do you always act awkward when I ask questions about my family or magic?"

"Sarin, I think that's enough," Fallon blurted out.

"No, sister, it's fine. Sarin has a right to know."

Farrow and Fallon exchanged a heated glance before Farrow cleared her throat. "Your father was a member of one of the most powerful covens in our known history, and from what we've managed to piece together, they were not the nicest people. Years ago, their coven lived in the forest, on top of the very vortex you spoke of. Your grandmother went mad in her quest for power and attempted to use your aunt as a conduit to supply the coven with even more magic she siphoned from the vortex. When your aunt realized the truth, she turned against the coven and was responsible for the fire that killed your father and the rest of the elders. No one's been able to find the clearing the coven lived in, and no surviving members have re-surfaced since that horrible event. I know I lied to you, but I thought it was in your best interest, considering you never met your father. Better to think of him as a hero, but now I realize that wasn't my call to make. All this information is just speculation, Sarin, which is another reason I didn't want to share it with you."

Sarin was shocked by Farrow's honesty. "Thank you for the history lesson, but none of that explains why you know so much about my family if you've never met them?"

"I don't have to explain myself, but I'll offer you this out of respect for your friendship with my daughter. As an elder of my coven, I have a sworn duty to investigate what happens to other witches—especially lost witches who could cause big problems. If even one witch gets exposed, it could mean death by execution for all. So yes, I'm looking into what happened to the Delvaux Coven, and if I find anything, I will share it. But no, Sarin, I will not train you, no matter how many times you ask, because it's a liability. I will do what is best for Faith, and Fallon will do the same with the twins. I'm asking you to respect that and stop casting."

With that, Farrow excused herself from the table.

Pushing out her chair, Sarin bee-lined it for the front door, ignoring Faith's protests. There was nothing left to say. Farrow had thrown down the gauntlet. Stomping down the driveway, Sarin felt her face getting hot at the nerve of that woman. Sliding in behind the steering wheel, Sarin didn't see Faith coming around the back of the car until she flung open the passenger door and let herself inside.

"What in the hell are you doing? Get your ass back inside before she grounds you for life!"

"I'm trying to stop you from doing something stupid!" Faith shouted. "And I'm on your side!"

Resting her head against the steering wheel, Sarin tried to calm down. Faith was a good person regardless of her DNA and didn't deserve her wrath.

Faith placed a comforting hand on her back. "I had no idea she was looking for the vortex or information on your family. Shit, I didn't even know my mom was the head of our coven."

Faith's sad voice tamped down some of Sarin's anger.

"She's lying to us both. I can walk away if I want, but she's your mom, Faith."

"Yeah, I know. But it's time we did something about it, right?"

Intrigued, Sarin glanced at her friend like she was seeing her for the first time. "What did you have in mind?"

"Tonight, when she goes to bed, I'm going to steal her grimoire, and then we're going to find a spell that can help us figure this shit out."

As much as Sarin yearned for answers, she didn't want Faith to put herself on the chopping block. "I can't ask you to do that, Faith. You know she'll eventually find out, and then what?"

"I don't care. I'll be at your house with the book at midnight. Just let me in, and we'll go from there."

Faith jumped out of the car without another word, leaving Sarin equally scared and hopeful.

CHAPTER 5

A T TEN PAST MIDNIGHT, there was a hard knock on Sarin's front door. She wasn't surprised to find Faith on the other side, sweating like she'd just robbed a bank, but the two nervous-looking twins standing beside her were another story.

"What's with Tweedledee and Tweedledum?"

Faith smiled sheepishly. "I didn't have a choice. They threatened to wake my mom if I didn't bring them."

"We're tired of our mom ignoring us, too." Selene added, "And we think she used a potion or a spell to bind our powers. Every witch I've ever met has discovered their element by the time they reach our age, but we don't even have a tingle of magic."

Sarin felt terrible for all of them. Their elders were essentially cutting them off at the knees.

"Hurry up and get inside. Who knows how much time we have until Farrow realizes you stole the book? I'm sure it's got magical GPS on it or something."

Scurrying up the stairs, Faith threw the book on the bed before plopping down beside it. "I'm not sure where to start. This thing is hella thick."

Sarin's first thought was to look for a spell to locate a lost relative, but that felt too easy. Farrow hadn't been able to find her family, and Sarin assumed that self-riotous bitch would have used a locator spell the first time too. Then again, maybe she had, and it hadn't worked? After all, Farrow wasn't a Delvaux, and magic always came with a catch. Maybe a call from blood to blood would work for Sarin.

As Faith flipped through the pages in the grimoire, the room seemed to hum with power. "Do you want a truth spell? Something like that?"

"Are there any locator spells? Or a spell to form a connection with someone else? Or shit, let's get literal; a spell to find answers?"

After a few minutes of exploration, Faith's expression turned serious. "Nothing that specific, but there is a spell called Emptiness Reversal, which claims it can help you find a precious missing object."

"You sure there's nothing better?" Sarin asked. The spell wasn't spot on, but they could make it work with the right intention behind it.

"No. I don't think my mom updates this thing. None of these spells are even in her handwriting. Maybe she has other books I don't know about, but this is the only one I've ever seen her with."

"We want to help this time!" Selene demanded. "No more sitting on the sidelines, or we tell Mom!"

Sarin wanted to punch Selene in her stupid face, but she refrained by reminding herself the girl was just an immature teenager.

"Aren't you worried about what your mom will do to you when she finds out you helped Faith steal the book? I'd keep your mouth shut if I were you. And just so we're clear, you two can cast and close the circle but nothing else."

"Fine!" Selene huffed. "I'll go get the salt."

Phoebe followed her downstairs, and when they were out of earshot, Faith announced, "I know! I know! They're annoying, but we need the power boost for the spell."

"You know, you could have spelled them to sleep before you came over."

Faith rolled her eyes. "You know how bad my spells work on a good day, and who knows how long a sleep spell would've lasted? If they'd woken up twenty minutes in, my mom would already be here, taking the book back and locking me in my room forever. That could still happen, so stop giving me so much shit."

"Touché. Do we need any other ingredients?"

Faith scanned the page, using her finger as a guide. "Just an empty glass, but there's already one on your nightstand. It says the glass will serve as a symbolic container representing the emptiness you want to fill with the return of the missing article. So, it looks like we need the glass and salt."

Annoying giggling signaled the twin's return, and Phoebe entered the room, twirling the Morton can around in her hand like it was a magic wand.

"Focus!" Sarin snapped. "You're spilling it everywhere."

Phoebe flashed her a small, sheepish smile. "Sorry."

"I don't need your apology. I need you to pay attention to the job I asked you to do! If that's too hard, then you can wait downstairs."

Sprinting into action, the twins poured the salt into a perfect circle while Faith explained the rest of the spell.

"Once we begin, it says we have to focus and let the object we want most appear inside our minds, or your mind rather, Sarin. Then, once the spell is complete, it's supposed to manifest itself in real life. Sounds simple enough."

Sarin snorted. "But it never is, is it?"

The twins sat on the end of the bed and waited quietly for their next Que. Sarin felt torn over letting them be involved, but she knew the more power the spell had, the better chance of success. They would probably only get one shot at this before Farrow found out and magically grounded them for life, so it was now or never.

Focusing on the twins, who were both sitting still for once, Sarin softened. "Can you sit inside the circle with us and focus only on what I tell you?"

"Really?" Phoebe asked, her body vibrating with excitement.

Selene shot her some serious side-eye, clearly skeptical of the offer.

"Stop looking at me like that, Selene. If you want to help, come help."

Shrugging, Selene let her sister lead her inside of the ring of salt. Faith and Sarin followed with the grimoire in hand. Faith then set the book down in front of them and handed the empty glass to Sarin.

"The spell says you need to place the glass upside down in the middle of the circle and visualize the object you want to manifest, along with any feelings of emptiness surrounding it. Then, we chant the spell three times. When the spell is complete, leave the glass upside down until the object returns to you. It says if the object doesn't return within a week, it might be lost forever."

Joining hands with Faith, Sarin motioned for the twins to do the same. "Then let's hope it works. Girls, clear your minds and only focus on helping me find my object. Can you do that?"

The twins both nodded and then the four of them began to chant:

I have emptiness in a glass

An emptiness like the one I feel

Once the object returns to me

My emptiness will heal

Sarin conjured an image of her father inside her mind and sent all her wishes to the universe to fill the emptiness his absence had left in her soul. As they chanted, Sarin visualized meeting a member of her family. The face inside her mind was blank, but her intention was clear. After the third time through, a phantom wind blew through the room, knocking over the glass and rattling the mirror above Sarin's nightstand.

"Shit!" Faith yelled as she scrambled to turn the cup back over. "I hope that was a good sign."

Phoebe's eyes went wide. "Does that sort of thing normally happen when you cast?"

Faith's sigh was audible. "Honestly, I don't have a barometer for what's normal or not with magic just yet. Why don't you guys close the circle for me while I put the salt back."

Faith motioned for Sarin to follow her downstairs while the twins cleaned up.

"What is it?" Sarin asked, taking the stairs two by two.

"Didn't you feel that?"

"Feel what, exactly?" Sarin pressed. "I felt a warmth rush over me, but that's normal when we practice."

"I don't know. Something feels wrong."

Sarin knew stealing the book was a lot for Faith, but her extrasensory perception wasn't throwing off any alarms. "I think you might be a little paranoid about the book. Maybe it's coloring your emotions?"

"You're probably right," Faith said as she leaned against the counter.

"Thanks for letting us help," Selene called out as the twins jogged down the stairs.

"Wow. A thank you. Really?" Sarin joked. "Did you finish closing the circle?"

"Yes!" they chimed in unison. Even though they were twins, Sarin still found it creepy when they did shit like that.

"Good. Get that book back before Faith's mom notices anything is up."

As Sarin said goodbye to her friends, she didn't hear the guttural growl that echoed from inside her bedroom mirror. Unbeknownst to her, the twins hadn't properly closed the circle.

CHAPTER 6

Haven Hargrove felt the magical call wash over her like a warm winter blanket. She'd been searching the Algonquin National Park for almost two weeks, looking for any signs of her mother, but hadn't found shit since stepping through the watery portal that had brought her to this place. The lush clearing from her visions was now a charred and empty landscape, but the ground still hummed with ancient magic. Whoever had cast the summoning spell had called blood to blood. It could be a clue or a fucking trap.

Haven hadn't planned things out before leaping into the portal that had transported her from Florida to the wild wilderness of Canada in the blink of an eye. No, she'd been impulsive, and that tiny little error had cost her.

Her dad was livid, understandably, and she'd had no choice but to cast a spell on him over the phone to calm him down and let her borrow his credit card to rent a modest Airbnb a few miles outside the forest. It was not her proudest moment, but these were desperate times. Then, there was the small matter of spelling the park ranger into letting her commandeer his car with no questions asked.

Pulling her mother's grimoire out of her satchel bag, Haven ran her fingers across the symbol of the triangle embossed on its cover. The book felt like home, and she had to bite back the sting of tears that threatened to spill. She missed her dad and her friends. But this wasn't the time to get sentimental; right now, she needed to focus on casting a glamour and a solid protection spell before she followed the proverbial breadcrumbs back to whoever had summoned her. The call felt familial, but technically, she was related to everyone in her mother's coven, even the psychos, so she wasn't taking chances.

Changing her face was the easy part. She'd perfected this particular glamour spell a few years back, and now, transforming her fiery red locks into a sleek platinum blonde was as effortless as breathing. Next was a quick green-to-blue hue for her eyes and a tiny rounding of her nose to finish the look. The protection spell was a bit more complicated, so she needed to double-check her grimoire to ensure she remembered the wording correctly. The ancient tome was thick, and the pages felt crisp between her fingers as she flipped through them. She was looking for a spell to hide her aura. It was similar to a cloaking spell but worked better against magic wielders. It didn't take long to find the spell in question, and after going over the ingredient list, she was relieved to discover that she already had everything she needed to cast it. After mixing and grinding all the ingredients into a paste, Haven smeared the mixture over her heart and recited the words to the spell three times. When the spell was complete, she packed her tiny, worn backpack with the essentials and said goodbye to the small rental in case she didn't return. As Haven pulled her borrowed car onto Highway 60 toward Huntsville, she sensed this was all meant to be. The summoning spell was solid and bright, like a beacon calling her in the darkness.

CHAPTER 7

S ARIN CRASHED HARD THAT night. Usually, she slept peacefully, but tonight, a strange shadowy being plagued her dreams. Everywhere she turned, the shadow assumed the identity of the person closest to her. Malice and rage emanated from every visage it took, and they all had one purpose -to hurt her. Screaming, Sarin flung out a bright ball of light to extinguish the shadowy demon. The light ricocheted off its chest as the monster swept out its long claws and slashed her across the abdomen. Warm blood filled her hands as she tried to keep her internal organs from spilling out onto the dirty street. Blood bubbled up in her throat and escaped as a silent scream as the demon lunged for her.

Waking up in a terrified panic, Sarin clung to her pillow for comfort. Her throat was raw, like she'd been screaming in real life, and her hair was damp with sweat. Taking a big sip of water from the cup on her nightstand, Sarin sighed as the wet relief slid down her throat. Rubbing her hands across her stomach, she was grateful to be awake and alive. The glass cup was still sitting upside down in the middle of her room, and as Sarin got out of bed, she was careful to step around it. She still had six more days for the spell to take or tank, which felt like an eternity.

Pulling a clean t-shirt from her dresser, Sarin noticed the mirror that hung above it was a little off-kilter. The strange wind that had come through with the spell must have moved it. Reaching up to straighten it, she cringed at the sight of her reflection. She was the very definition of a hot mess. Pulling her curly red hair up into a messy bun, she froze when a weird ripple followed the movement of her arm in the mirror's surface. Leaning in, she waved her hands in front of the mirror, trying to repeat the strange occurrence, but nothing happened. Her phone chose that moment to chime, and her face flushed when she read who the text was from.

Alex: Been thinking about you. Can we meet at Lions Lookout to talk? Tonight?

Without thinking, she responded: that's a big h-to-the-no!

If Alex thought she would meet him at the make-out capital of Huntsville after all this time, then he was insane. Staring at the phone in her hand, Sarin realized she was waiting for his reply and immediately shut the stupid thing off. She hated that he still affected her so much. Grabbing what she needed for class, Sarin didn't notice that her mirror image stayed in place long after she left.

CHAPTER 8

WHEN FAITH DIDN'T SHOW up for class, Sarin felt sick. Cue the anxiety spiral. Pulling out her phone, she turned it back to find a missed text from Faith explaining she was skipping class to catch up on sleep. Relief flooded her, and she thanked the goddess, or whoever, that Faith was okay. There was also another unread text from Alex.

Alex: Please stop ignoring me. I'm trying to do the right thing, for once.

Fine. Fine. Fine, Sarin thought. The spell said it would bring answers, so maybe meeting Alex was step number one. If she was being honest with herself, her gut instinct was screaming that she should go, and she never denied her sense of intuition.

Hoping she was right and not just giving herself an excuse to see him, she texted back.

7:00 PM. Don't be late.

He responded with a smiley face emoji.

On the way home, Sarin contemplated driving by Faith's house to check on her in person. Farrow was an evil bitch on a good day, and Sarin wouldn't put it past her to hijack Faith's phone and send out fake texts about her status. What if the crazy witch already had Faith on lockdown? Ignoring her insane thoughts, Sarin tuned into her extrasensory perception instead. Picturing Faith's face inside her mind, she focused on her friend's energy signature and felt nothing but a sense of peace. That small comfort helped her let go of the worry for the moment.

It was time to refocus on the present, and since she'd been neglecting her homework for the past few days, she desperately needed to play catch-up before meeting Alex. Spreading her school books across the dining room table, Sarin cued up her favorite Indie playlist and dove into her anatomy homework. She was getting into the section on endocrinology when she heard a loud *thump* upstairs. Pausing the music, she waited for a few seconds, and when there were no other discernable noises, she dismissed it as a bird or rogue squirrel. A few minutes later, another thump-thump rang out. Annoyed and slightly concerned this time, she decided to check on the situation. Pausing her music for a second time, she slid her iPhone

into the back pocket of her jeans before tip-toeing up the stairs. *Thump.*
Thump. Thump.

Three this time. And the noise was coming from inside her bedroom.
She thought about calling 911 but stopped herself. What if this had
something to do with the spell? What if the person she called was waiting
for her in her room? Pushing past the fear, Sarin opened her bedroom door
and was completely confused when she found the room empty.

Directing her annoyance at the cup on the floor, she proclaimed, "I wish
you'd just do your job! All this waiting is making me feel insane!"

She didn't have time for a mental breakdown right now, so she took a
quick shower before the meet-up to keep herself occupied. The humidity
in the bathroom made her skin all dewy, so after towel-drying her hair, she
headed back into her room to apply her makeup in the mirror above her
dresser. Once her eyeliner was on point, and her lips were tinted in a shade
of red that matched her hair, Sarin took a step back to survey her work and
immediately dropped her makeup bag. Her eyes, usually a bright shade of
green, were now pitch black in her reflection. Leaning in, Sarin wiped her
hand across the mirror to see if something was on the glass, distorting the
reflection. When her skin met the glass, it burned. Yanking her hand back,
Sarin stared at the small red welt swelling on her palm. Confused, she dared
to look back at her reflection to find that her eyes were their normal color
once again.

Shaking, Sarin ran into the hallway and called Faith.

"Where have you been? I was worried when you didn't text me back this morning."

Breathing heavily, Sarin let the comfort of Faith's voice wash over her.

"Sarin? Are you there? Is everything okay?"

"Sorry, yeah, I'm here. And I'm sorry I didn't text you back. Alex was blowing up my phone, and I shut it off while I was in class."

"Why do you sound so out of breath? Talk to me?"

"When you left last night, you said something felt wrong. Do you still feel that way?"

"I felt a lot of things last night. But you were right; it was mainly terror over being caught. Why? Did something happen? Did the spell work?"

"I still don't know if the spell worked, but I heard weird sounds inside my room. And I swear my eyes turned black when I looked at myself in the mirror."

"You know there are always side effects from casting. Why don't I come over, and we can do a cleansing spell to eliminate any bad juju the spell may have left behind?"

"That's a good idea, but I already agreed to meet Alex at The Lookout."

"You did what? Why?" Faith yelled into the phone.

"He said he's trying to make amends or some shit. And since our stupid spell called to fill an emptiness in my soul, I thought it might be worth it to go. Honesty, I don't know why I said yes, but can you please meet me back here around nine?"

"Fine. But I expect you to spill all the tea later."

"Agreed."

After ending the call, Sarin realized she wasn't happy with her outfit, but until Faith came over to do the cleansing spell, there was no way she was going back to her room. Reminding herself again that she didn't care what Alex thought about her or her fashion choices, she left to find out what her ex had to say.

CHAPTER 9

IT WAS PROUD OF itself. Not only had it changed the girl's reflection, but it had burned the stupid bitch, too. Pacing in its void, it felt a ripple of pain undulate through its body. It now had a name for its agony. Hunger. And there was nothing to consume in this space. Pausing in front of the floating square it now knew was a mirror, it pushed on the glass and was surprised when the surface gave way, expanding like a piece of plastic into the room beyond. Testing the limits, it realized it could bend the glass to extreme lengths but not break it. The glass conformed around its spindly arm like a movable glove, and on the second try, it managed to grip the blanket on the bed before the fabric slipped from its glass-coated fingers. Its prison held steady, but now it had a weapon. It would convince the witch to let it out, and then she would be the first one it would consume.

It was a fitting reward for its creator.

CHAPTER 10

S ARIN PULLED INTO THE parking lot at Lions Lookout promptly at seven to find Alex leaning against the hood of his red pickup truck. The view of the Muskoka River on this side of the lookout was beautiful, especially at sunset. Between the strange happenings at her house and the fluttering feeling Alex always invoked, Sarin felt like she might vomit on her sneakers. Taking a moment to center herself, she waved to Alex before exiting the car. His posture was relaxed as he watched her approach. Sarin joined him, taking the spot to his right, but kept her gaze locked on the sunset.

"Last time we were here, it was under very different circumstances," Alex stated.

"Yeah, well, things change when you only think with your penis."

Alex's posture went rigid. "I deserved that."

"And a lot more!" Sarin added.

"Look, I didn't come here to fight. I just wanted to say thank you."

Shocked, Sarin finally looked over at him and saw the honest regret in his eyes. "Thank you for what?"

"Before I met you, I was in a bad place. I never told you this, but I used to use drugs. Like, a lot of hard drugs. I was up and down for a long time after rehab, but when I met you, I finally felt steady. You always supported everything I did—especially all the business stuff with my brother. We had a rough childhood, which I also never told you about, and thankfully, my brother found healthier ways to cope. Me, not so much. Anyway, that's not the point. Look, my biggest problem is that I need to feel in control constantly, and Sarin, I fell in love with you so fast that it made me feel the opposite."

Sarin didn't think she could handle the heaviness of this conversation, but as she raised her hand to pause him, he silenced her.

"Wait, please. I need to get this out. I needed to feel in control, so I cheated. I cheated to try to convince myself I didn't need you so much. It's not an excuse. I just wanted to clear the air because, contrary to what you believe, I do love you and want you to know the truth before you make up your mind about me. I'm not asking you to reconsider dating me, but I'd like to be friends. I know I still have a lot of work to do on myself before I can make anyone else happy."

Sarin was trying to pay attention to Alex's bleeding heart moment, but she got distracted when she caught sight of a brunette a few cars down who looked a hell of a lot like Phoebe. The girl in question was busy making out with a boy that was way too old for her, and Sarin knew this for a fact because the asshat on the other end of the lip-lock went to school with her. Storming away from Alex mid-conversation, Sarin knocked on the window of the silver BMW. Of course, the douchebag drove an expensive car. He probably thought he was entitled enough to take advantage of underage girls, too. Phoebe jumped away from him at the sound of the loud rapping.

"Get out of the car, Phoebe!"

Mr. D-Bag rolled down the window on Phoebe's side and shot Sarin the middle finger. "I don't know who you are, but why don't you go fuck right off."

Smiling, Sarin leaned into the open window so he could see her face. "I'm the person who will only give you one warning. Phoebe is only sixteen, but I'm sure you already knew that."

Taking out her phone, Sarin snapped a quick picture of the pedophile with Phoebe in the car with him.

"Look, bitch!" the man-child growled as he swung open his car door. "You don't know what you're talking about. She said she was legal. Now delete that fucking picture."

"Fat chance, asshole."

The guy advanced on her, and even though Sarin was perfectly capable of taking care of herself, she didn't mind when Alex stepped in.

"Step away from her if you know what's good for you!" Alex warned.

"Get out of the car, or I'm calling your mom."

Huffing like the child she was, Phoebe begrudgingly obeyed.

"You're one to talk!" D-Bag shouted at Alex, "With all the tail you pull in this town."

"You mean all the legal tail? This is low, even for you, Blake."

Sarin made a mental note that D-Bag's name was Blake. He'd be much easier to cyber-stalk now if he didn't heed her warning to stay away from Phoebe.

"Fuck you, Alex!" Blake seethed before getting back into his car and speeding away.

"Phoebe, what in the hell were you thinking?"

"You have eyes," Phoebe stated with a shrug.

"Did you plan on having sex with him? Because that's what guys like that are after when they prey on young girls."

Phoebe's face turned tomato red. "No! I don't know; this was our first date."

"Let me give you a piece of advice. Any guy, even an age-appropriate one, who takes their first date to Lions Lookout doesn't have good intentions in mind. Don't set yourself up for a bad outcome, Phoebe. There are horrible people in this world."

Phoebe nodded as a tear slid down her cheek.

"Can you wait by my car while I say goodbye to Alex?"

Phoebe turned around and headed for the car without another word.

"I guess it's my turn for a thank you," Sarin announced once Phoebe was out of earshot.

"For my apology or intervention?" Alex asked.

"Both," Sarin said sheepishly. "And for sharing all that stuff with me. I know it took a lot to open up, and I'll keep that information between us."

Alex leaned in and gave her a light hug. "I'm just glad I got to say it all, and now that we're officially friends, don't be a stranger."

"Friends," Sarin repeated out loud and meant it. It was time to put his painful chapter of her life behind her.

CHAPTER II

P HOEBE DIDN'T UTTER A word on the drive back, and Sarin was
grateful for the silence. She just prayed the girl took her advice and
stayed away from creepy ass Blake.

"Faith is meeting me at the house and can take you home after we finish
a quick cleansing spell."

"Why do you need a cleansing spell? Did something go wrong?"

Pulling into the driveway, Sarin glanced at her bedroom window with
trepidation. "Honestly, Pheebs? I don't know. I heard strange noises
coming from inside my bedroom earlier, and I want to cover our bases."

Sarin omitted the part about her reflection changing and the burn on
her palm. There was no reason to cause a sixteen-year-old any additional

anxiety. Phoebe visibly shivered as they entered the house through the kitchen door, and Sarin wasn't surprised. The girl only wore a tiny tank top and shorts that were way too short, even by today's standards.

"Why don't we head upstairs, and you can pick out one of my sweaters to borrow? I can tell you're freezing."

Sarin was hesitant to go into her room without Faith, but offering Phoebe a little comfort after a rough night was the least she could do. Phoebe followed her up the stairs and ran face-first into her back when she froze. Sarin's bedroom looked like a war zone. Her framed photographs lay in broken piles all over the floor, and her dresser drawers were pulled open with clothes spilling out everywhere.

"Wow, Sarin. What happened in here?" Phoebe asked as she sidestepped out from behind her.

Sarin put her hand out to stop Phoebe from fully entering the room just as a hideous laugh rang out. Glancing across her room toward the mirror and the source of the sound, Sarin jumped when her reflection smiled back at her.

"Phoebe, back away slowly," Sarin warned.

"What the fuck is that?" Phoebe asked with a gasp.

Sarin's reflection hissed at them.

"Who are you?" Sarin demanded.

"Who do you think I am? You created me."

Sarin stared at her distorted reflection in confusion.

"The spell, witch, remember?" her reflection spat with disdain. "You called me into existence, and now I'm here. If you want the answers you seek, all you have to do is let me out."

"It's lying," Phoebe whispered.

Sarin knew that, but she needed time to think. "I cast a spell to find my family. And clearly, we're not related. So, how do I know you have any information I want or need?"

Her reflection morphed into a ghostly version of herself with onyx-colored eyes, pale skin, and hollowed-out cheeks. "You have to trust. Why would I be here if I'm not the one you called for?"

Good point, Sarin thought, but all her witchy vibes screamed not to trust this thing. "True, but sometimes, you have to give a little to get a little. Tell me something about my family that will convince me you have the knowledge you claim?"

As Sarin spoke to her creepy likeness inside the mirror, she gently nudged Phoebe into the hallway.

Her reflection flashed her a smile that was full of malice. "If you want something in this world, you just have to take it."

Before Sarin could blink, a spindly grey hand shot out from inside the mirror and wrapped its fingers around her throat. Her feet dragged on the carpet and debris as the evil entity pulled her across the room toward the glass. "I will kill you and everyone you care about if you don't let me out! Swear to it, and I'll let go."

Sarin felt its fetid breath fan out across her face as she struggled in its grip.

"Never!" she choked out.

Its fingers dug in harder. "I will find a way out, just like I found a way through, and when I do, I'll enjoy ripping out your spine."

Fire erupted around the mirror, and the entity released Sarin with a shriek. Falling, she landed on the ground in an awkward pile. Disoriented, Sarin looked up to find Faith standing in the doorway with smoke wafting from her palms. Faith's blonde hair was singed at the ends, and she was white as a ghost. Sarin tried to stand, but a sharp pain shot down her right leg. Shifting her weight to the left side, she managed to limp her way into the hallway.

Slamming the bedroom door shut, Sarin sat down at the top of the stairs, panting.

"Holy shit, Faith! You just shot fire from your hands!" Phoebe announced with a shocked look on her face.

Faith was still staring down at her hands in awe. "I saw that thing choking Sarin, and it just happened."

Sarin wanted to celebrate Faith's newfound power, but they had bigger issues. "Do you guys have any idea what that thing was? Or what the fuck we're going to do about it?"

"The reflection looked just like you, even when it changed," Phoebe commented.

"So?" Sarin asked, motioning for them to move farther from the door.

"So," Phoebe added, "Haven't you seen The Vampire Diaries? I'm binge-watching it right now, but that's not important. My point is, since it looks like you, maybe it's your doppelgänger."

"Did she hit her head when she was a baby?" Sarin asked Faith in all seriousness.

"Nope," Faith said with a smirk. "She's just special."

Phoebe crossed her arms over her chest. "Make fun of me all you want, but at least look into it. Okay? It's a thing."

"Fine," Sarin caved. "You can help me do that later. Right now, we need a way to seal that fucking door."

Faith pulled a small piece of paper out of her back pocket. "Maybe we don't have to seal it. I took a little sneak peek in my mom's grimoire again to find the cleansing spell you asked for, and technically speaking, this spell should cleanse the house of that thing since it's the bad juju we want to eliminate. Right? Do you have any sage?"

"Faith, I don't think a little sage is going to cut it." Sarin snapped. "We need to use the big guns for this."

"It's not just sage. It's sage magnified by the spell."

"All my magical supplies are inside that room, so we're screwed."

"I have some at home, but once I go back, there's no way my mom will let me leave again," Phoebe added, trying to be helpful.

"Faith, can you drive Phoebe home, grab it, and come right back?"

"And leave you here all alone? No way!" Faith protested.

"If it breaks out before you get back, I'll run, okay? Phoebe's house is only fifteen minutes away. Ten if you speed."

Faith took Phoebe by the arm and flashed Sarin a disapproving look as they walked down the stairs. Sarin's leg was still on fire, so she had to rely on the railing for help.

"You can barely walk. How do you expect to run if that thing gets out?"

Faith was right, but they didn't have a plan B, "Just be quick, so I don't have to worry about it!"

Closing the front door behind her friends, Sarin stared at her bedroom door with trepidation; this would be the longest thirty minutes of her life. Hobbling into the dining room, she grabbed her laptop off the table and set up shop at the bottom of the stairs so she could keep an eye on her bedroom door. There was nothing to do but wait and worry, so she decided to research Phoebe's theory. All the lore she found online described doppelgängers as monstrous humanoid creatures known for their shape-shifting abilities. That made sense since the thing in the mirror had taken on Sarin's appearance. The lore also explained that in their true form, doppelgängers appeared as tall, gray-skinned beings with hairless bodies and human-shaped eyes that lacked pupils. The arm that shot out of her mirror had been scaly and gray so that also tracked. The hand-drawn illustration next to the description made Sarin's skin crawl. Even if the thing in her mirror was a doppelgänger, it still didn't explain why it was in there or how to get rid of it. Another website claimed doppelgängers were immune to mind-affecting spells, and once they killed and shape-shifted into another person, they could detect the thoughts of their victims and mimic them. A shiver ran down Sarin's spine at the thought of a creature with that kind of power.

Reading on, Sarin finally found a passage that put everything into perspective. That being said, the site was a fandom-type website and not a reliable source of information. But didn't all lore originate from some sprinkle of the truth? She was a living, breathing witch, so maybe all this shit was the real deal. The text explained that, theoretically, any witch who performed a spell incorrectly could be cursed with a doppelgänger as punishment. Thinking back to the night they performed the Emptiness Reversal spell, Sarin couldn't recall a single step they'd missed. Faith had suspected something was off, though, and that strange wind had blown straight into the mirror. Regardless of the whys, she now had an angry doppelgänger trapped inside her mirror and no way to get rid of it. A loud crack rang out from upstairs as if the monster was reading her thoughts.

Scrambling to her feet, Sarin was horrified to see a large fissure forming down the center of her bedroom door.

Pulling out her phone, she texted Faith: hurry!!!!!!

Faith's response was almost immediate: 5 minutes away

Thank god, Sarin thought.

CHAPTER 12

F AITH BARRELED THROUGH THE front door like her feet were on fire, and Sarin had never been happier to see her. Dumping the contents of her purse out on the floor, Faith quickly sifted through the pile until she found what she needed. Unfolding the spell, Faith's hand visibly shook as she lit one end of the sage.

"Repeat these words with me three times,"

I banish the darkness from this place

Clear out the wrongness in this space

With love and light, end this pain

And make this space safe once again

A loud growl reverberated from above them, and Sarin focused all her magical intention on removing the doppelgänger from her mirror.

By the third time through, Sarin was sweating from the exertion. "Do you think it worked?"

"You know we have to go in there to be sure," Faith declared while wiping off her equally sweat-soaked forehead.

Using the railing to help her stand, Sarin hesitated. "Do you think you can conjure your fire again if we need it?"

"Fingers crossed."

Tip-toeing up the stairs, Sarin paused to press her ear against the splintered wooden door. "I don't hear anything. Are you ready?"

Faith answered with a firm nod before Sarin slowly pushed open the door. The wall surrounding the mirror was charred to a crisp, but everything else looked the same: a total wreck, but the same.

"My reflection looks normal, but it might just be fucking with us."

"True." Faith agreed. "But if its goal was to be set free and it's still stuck, then it will have to make a re-appearance."

Sarin wasn't convinced it was gone. It all felt too easy. "I think I'm going to clean up and sleep downstairs on the couch tonight."

"I'll stay with you," Faith offered as she picked up the rumpled comforter from the floor.

Sarin was grateful for Faith's offer. It was hard to admit, but Sarin didn't want to be alone in this house. "Thanks, babe."

An hour later, Sarin was exhausted and sprawled out on one end of the oversized sectional, with Faith snuggled up at her feet. Her room was still in shambles, but at least they'd put a dent in the cleanup with no signs of the doppelgänger. Taking a deep, calming breath, Sarin closed her eyes. She still felt unsettled, but her weary body won out over her intrusive thoughts, and she quickly fell into a deep sleep.

Her dreams were frantic, with one scene bleeding into the next. First, she saw a girl about her age with bright red hair fighting against a mirror image of herself. Behind the girl, a gorgeous man lounged on a gigantic brick chair that radiated with power, but he looked utterly bored. The man noticed Sarin watching him and smiled. His smile looked sweet, but a sense of unfathomable evil washed over Sarin when they locked eyes. The man nodded as if he'd heard her thoughts and agreed with her assessment. Pulled from that scene, Sarin then dreamt of her mother. It was a typical morning, and Sarin watched her mom mill around the kitchen, making coffee and humming while she made breakfast. Overcome with a feeling of rage, Sarin pulled a knife from the butcher block and sliced it across her mother's throat. Blood sprayed, covering the pristine white countertops in a sea of red. Dream Sarin laughed as she watched her mother's dying body sink to the floor.

Sarin woke up to the sounds of her screams.

"It was just a dream. I'm right here," Faith called out.

Grabbing onto Faith, Sarin wailed, "She died! MY MOM DIED, AND I KILLED HER! Oh God, Faith, it felt so real!"

"Do you want to talk about it?"

Sniffling, Sarin pulled back. "Not really. I just hope that fucking thing in the mirror is gone for good!"

Glancing at her watch, Faith cursed. "Class starts in an hour, and I can't miss another one. Mr. H already has it out for me. What do you want to do?"

"If I sit alone in this house all day, I might go crazy. My mom won't be back until tomorrow, so we should recheck my room for now, and if everything feels okay, I'll go with you.

"I have to swing by my house to change before we head to class, so why don't you just grab some clothes and get ready at my house?"

"Thanks, Faith. I don't know what I'd do without you."

"Good thing you never have to find out."

Satisfied the doppelgänger hadn't returned, Sarin left the house in Faith's car, unaware of the person who passed them on the street, riding in an Uber.

CHAPTER 13

"SARIN, ARE YOU HOME?" Lynne called out. "I got back early and took an Uber from the airport."

As Sarin's mother pulled her suitcase in through the back door, she immediately took notice of the messy blankets scattered across the sofa. The scene seemed out of place since Sarin never slept on the couch and rarely had friends over.

Confused, Lynne headed upstairs and got scared when she saw a large crack in the center of Sarin's bedroom door. Opening it up, she felt a sense of relief wash over her when she found her daughter safely asleep in her bed.

Sitting up, Sarin rubbed her sleepy eyes. "Hey, Mom. You're back early."

"Hi, sweetie. I didn't mean to wake you, but what in the hell happened to your door?"

"Yeah, about that. Do you mind giving me a second to wake up, and then we can talk about it downstairs?"

"Sure. I'll go down and make some coffee. I could use a cup."

Cleaning out the coffee pot, Lynne felt happy to be home. Even though Sarin was an adult, she still worried about her when she was away. It was the never-ending crutch of being a mother. Humming one of her favorite songs, Lynne smiled when she heard Sarin's footsteps coming down the stairs. Holding a steaming cup of coffee, Lynne turned around to offer it to her daughter and froze. The person standing before her looked like Sarin but also didn't. It was hard to explain, but Lynne knew everything about her daughter's face, and the face staring back at her was wrong somehow. Faking a smile because she didn't know what else to do, Lynne extended the coffee mug to the thing that looked like her child. Sarin not Sarin took a drink and immediately spit the liquid back into the cup.

"Is something wrong with the coffee?" Lynne asked while inching her way closer to the back door.

The thing that looked like Sarin shook its head as it pulled a kitchen knife from the butcher's block on the counter. Twirling the knife in the air, it stalked toward her.

Speaking in a distorted version of her daughter's voice, it crooned, "The coffees fine. I'm just in the mood for something else."

CHAPTER 14

SARIN WASN'T CONFIDENT SHE was going to pass this semester. Staring down at the questions on the pop quiz, she felt like a deer in headlights. She'd had zero time to study or catch up on homework with the shit-show that was her life. Circling as many answers as possible in the time allotted, she prayed her educated guesses would earn her a passing grade.

After turning in the quiz to Mr. H, Sarin excused herself to use the restroom. Turning on the faucet, she let the warm water pool in her hands for a few seconds before splashing it on her face. She needed to get her anxiety under control before her entire life came crashing down. Nothing had seemed out of place when she and Faith had checked on her bedroom earlier that morning, but Sarin had a nagging feeling the doppelgänger wasn't done with her. What if it was here to punish her like the lore suggested? What if the spell was a flop? Technically, she still had a few more days before the spell was set to manifest or fail, but having a doppelgänger trapped inside her mirror was a bad sign. Shooting a quick text to Phoebe and Selene, she asked the twins to meet her at her house after class. She wanted to go over the spell in detail to figure out what went wrong. If the doppelgänger did return, Faith would have to steal Farrow's spell book again, or they'd be forced to admit what they'd done and beg for her help. Cringing over the second option, Sarin prayed Faith's cleansing spell had done its job. Walking out of the bathroom, Sarin found Faith waiting by the classroom door.

"I bombed that quiz," Faith announced in a defeated voice.

"Hey, if we both fail, we can repeat year two together. Speaking of shitty life problems, I asked Selene and Phoebe to meet us at my house. I researched doppelgängers like Phoebe suggested, and as it turns out, they can be a by-product of bad spell casting. I know I didn't fuck up that spell, so we need to figure out what happened."

"Wonderful!" Faith said sarcastically.

A feeling of dread washed over Sarin as she and Faith pulled into the driveway. Selene's car was parked on the street, but the twins were nowhere to be seen. Sarin panicked and jumped out of the car without putting it in park.

"What the fuck, Sarin?" Faith yelled as she scrambled over the center console and into the driver's side seat to stop the car from rolling into the street.

"How'd they get inside?" Sarin screamed as she barreled toward the back door. "I locked the door!"

Fumbling for her keys, Sarin trembled as she unlocked the door.

"Oh, hi, honey! I'm so glad you're home," her mom said warmly.

It took a minute for Sarin's brain to catch up with the very ordinary, non-emergent scene inside the kitchen. Selene was busy cutting up vegetables while Phoebe poured an array of seasonings into a large mixing bowl.

"The twins are helping me make my famous spaghetti sauce."

"It's okay! They're safe!" Sarin shouted as Faith ran up behind her.

"I'm sorry if we scared you. I got back early this morning, and the girls said you asked them to meet you here. Didn't you read my texts?"

Sarin didn't remember seeing any texts, but she'd been distracted all morning. Ignoring the question, Sarin walked into the kitchen and pulled her mom in for a big hug. "I'm just happy you're home and making me dinner. Uber Eats is stealing all my money."

"Well, whose fault is that? You know how to cook."

"Knowing and liking are two different things," Sarin quipped.

Smiling, Lynne gestured toward Faith. "Can you take Selene to the garage with you and grab a few extra folding chairs to fit everyone at the table? Oh, and Sarin, do you mind grabbing the long tablecloth for me? It's inside the buffet cabinet in the living room."

"I know where we keep it, Mom."

"Oh, sorry. Since you never cook, I thought you might have forgotten."

Snorting, Sarin walked into the living room. "If you ever wonder where I get my sarcasm from, just take a long, hard look in the mirror."

Lynne laughed before putting the last of them to work. "Phoebe, do you mind grabbing another garlic container from the pantry? I think the sauce needs a little more."

Phoebe let out a blood-curdling scream that had Sarin running back to the kitchen.

"Phoebe, what is it?" Sarin asked as she came to an abrupt halt behind her friend.

"I don't understand," Phoebe mumbled. "She's here, but she's there. No, no, no!"

Taking Phoebe by the arm, Sarin lightly pulled the girl out of the way so she could see what was in the pantry. Sarin saw the feet first, bloodied and lying in a twisted, unnatural position. Then, as her eyes tracked up the body, she saw a sight that stole her breath. Her mother's lifeless body was sprawled out on the floor of the pantry, surrounded by a pool of blood. Her beautiful face was colorless, and she had a gaping slash across her stomach.

"Surprise!" an evil voice called out from behind them. "I'm still here, and poor Mommy Dearest didn't notice I wasn't you until it was too late."

Sarin wanted to crumble into a ball of grief right then and there, but acting on instinct, she spun around to face the doppelgänger that still looked like her mother.

Laughing, it slashed out at her with a knife, slicing a thick cut across Sarin's arm. "Now, let's have some fun now! Shall we?"

CHAPTER 15

"**P**HOEBE, I NEED YOU to run!" Sarin yelled, trying to block her friend from the monster before them.

Phoebe took one look at the doppelgänger and bolted for the kitchen door. Sarin was grateful the teen had been smart enough to listen for once.

"How'd you get out?" Sarin spat as she tried to apply pressure to her bleeding arm.

"Since you refused to help me, I found another way. I can mimic powers and appearances, and when I touched you, I replicated your magic for a short time and spelled myself out. Thanks for that."

Sarin wanted to fight, but the doppelgänger still looked like her mom, and it was messing with her head, "Pick a different body!"

The doppelgänger smirked at her. "I can't do that until I kill someone else. Are you volunteering?"

"Fuck you! What do you want?"

"Ah, right to the point. Hmm, what do I want? Right now, I want to feed, fuck, and kill, but not necessarily in that order. You gave me this life, and I plan to live it fully. Right after I kill you and permanently steal your magic."

Faith, Selene, and Phoebe chose that moment to reappear in the doorway, and Sarin cursed. Phoebe hadn't left; she'd only gone to the garage for reinforcements. Faith came in first, armed and ready with a fireball that she blasted straight at the doppelgänger.

It held up its hand and deflected the ball of flame like it was nothing. "Nice try. How do you like this?"

The doppelgänger clapped its hands together and sent out an energy blast that plowed Faith down like she was nothing but a blade of grass. Flailing, her friend fell backward before hitting her head on the countertop and crashing to the floor.

Charging the thing with a bravery that was both impressive and stupid, Selene barely made it two steps before her body froze in mid-stride. With no way to protect herself, Selene was helpless as the doppelgänger raised its knife and sliced it across her throat. The scene was a warped version of Sarin's dream and the very thing her underdeveloped powers were trying to warn her about. Phoebe knelt beside her sister, hysterically crying, as a rush of white-hot energy rose inside Sarin's body. The power felt foreign, but going on instinct, Sarin poured all her intention into getting the doppelgänger away from them, and as soon as the thought solidified in her mind, a bright burst of light shot out from her hand and hit the monster dead in its chest.

The doppelgänger's body seemed to move without its permission, taking choppy, frantic steps away from them. Between gritted teeth, it taunted, "Finally learning how to use those powers, are we? Well, this won't hold me for long."

Grabbing Phoebe by the chin, Sarin forced the girl to look away from her sister. Staring into Phoebe's misty gray eyes, Sarin saw a mix of grief and rage that broke her heart. "We can't do anything more for Selene, but you can still help Faith. Get out of this house and call your mother! Tell her what we did, and ask her to send help. It's the only way. Go! Now!"

When Phoebe didn't move, Sarin slapped her across the face. "Go, Phoebe. I'll hold it off as long as I can."

Phoebe's hand shook as she pulled the car keys out of Selene's front pocket.

Sarin looked up to find the doppelgänger slowly inching its way back toward them.

"GO. PHOEBE. NOW!"

After one last mournful look at her sister, Phoebe finally ran out the back door.

The doppelgänger shook off the last remnant of magic and was in front of Sarin faster than she could have anticipated. Grabbing her by the neck with a hand still shaped like her mother's, it squeezed.

"No one left to save you!" it sneered.

Gasping for air, Sarin fought under the pressure of its grip. She kicked and flailed, but it was no use. The doppelgänger increased the pressure until Sarin saw stars twinkling in and out of her line of sight.

"I'm really going to enjoy wearing your skin," it crooned. "Thank you for the gift of life. Now you can die for it."

Sarin felt a sense of calm wash over her as her body was deprived of oxygen. If Heaven were real, she'd see her mom again. And if death was nothing but an endless void, then nothing mattered. Surrendering to the inevitable, Sarin was confused when the pressure on her neck subsided. Falling, she hit the ground with a hard thud. Opening her eyes from her not-so-comfy horizontal position on the floor, Sarin saw the doppelgänger cowering before a blonde woman, who was donned in all black. The woman was chanting in a language Sarin didn't understand, and when she finished the spell, the doppelgänger blinked out of existence. At least, that's what it looked like; Sarin's vision was still a little blurry. Pushing herself up to a seated position, Sarin watched with nervous anticipation as the stranger turned around to face her. Long blonde hair framed a petite face with icy blue eyes. Eyes that bore into Sarin's with a familiarity that confused her. Walking toward her, the stranger crouched until they were at eye level.

Smiling warmly, the stranger said, "Hello, cousin. I got your message."

CHAPTER 16

As Sarin stared into her savior's icy blue eyes, it took her a minute to realize the woman was talking about the spell.

"It's not every day you see a doppelgänger. I think we have a lot to talk about, cousin. I'm Haven, by the way," she said, offering her hand.

Sarin took it and let Haven help her stand up. "Shit! Faith!"

"Your friend will be fine. She has a concussion but nothing more," Haven said softly. "I'm sorry I didn't get here in time to save the other one."

As Sarin knelt before her best friend, she pushed the blood-soaked hair from her face. Daring a glance at Selene, Sarin's tears finally fell in a tsunami of grief and pain. This was all her fault. She'd sacrificed her mother and her friends in her quest for answers.

"All magic comes with a cost. Often, the price is too high," Haven announced like she was reading Sarin's thoughts.

"What the fuck do you know?" Sarin snapped.

The sadness on Haven's face was palpable, "More than you can imagine, cousin,"

Coughing, Faith finally began to stir.

Pulling her in for a hug, Sarin whispered. "I'm right here. I got you."

"What happened? And who is that?" Faith asked when her eyes landed on Haven.

Sarin held her breath for what was coming.

"Oh my god, Selene? Selene!"

Faith pulled away from Sarin and crawled to her cousin's body on her hands and knees.

"She died trying to save us," Sarin said, but the words felt all wrong. How could Selene be gone? How could her mother be gone? This had to be another nightmare.

"What happened to her? And where's Phoebe?" Faith asked with bated breath.

"After the doppelgänger attacked you, Selene went after it. It still had the knife, and I couldn't stop her in time. I got Phoebe out before it strangled me, but I couldn't protect Selene."

"Phoebe's safe?"

Sarin nodded, fumbling for the right words. "I'm so sorry, Faith! This is all my fault. I couldn't stop it, and after it hurt Selene, I told Phoebe to run for help."

Faith sat back on her butt, halfway between Sarin and Selene's body, with a weighted expression Sarin had never seen before. "It's not your fault, but my mom won't see it that way."

Sarin hadn't considered the repercussions of calling in the cavalry; she'd only wanted to save Faith and Phoebe. "Shit!"

"And who the fuck is that?" Faith asked again.

Haven was the picture of calm as she casually leaned against the counter. "I'm her cousin and the one you called for in the spell."

Faith shot Haven some major side eye, "And why should we believe you?"

"You do have eyes, yes?" Haven asked sarcastically, motioning between her and Sarin. "We look alike."

"You're joking. You look nothing like Sarin."

"Oh," Haven said with a smirk. "The glamour. Here, is this better?"

Haven's blonde hair bled through with red streaks until it was a full-on mass of scarlet. Then, her blue eyes transformed into a vivid shade of green.

Faith's gasp was audible. "Holy shit. You really do look alike."

"Seems the red hair runs in the family," Haven stated. "Sarin, I think it's time to go."

Sarin heard Haven's words, but her head was spinning. "Go where?"

"Do you want to explain it to her, or should I?" Haven proposed to Faith.

Faith scooted closer to Sarin. "She's right, Sarin. You have to go. My mom is coming, and once she figures out what happened here, you'll be a target."

"I can protect you and help you find the answers about our family that we've both been looking for," Haven proclaimed.

Sarin didn't know what to think. "What about my mom? I can't just leave her body in the pantry!"

"I'll take care of her," Faith promised, "But you have to go. I love you too much to let them hurt you."

Now, it was Sarin's turn to sob. "How do I know you'll be safe? Haven, what did you do to the doppelgänger?"

"I banished it, but I have no idea how long the spell will last on one of its kind. We can find a more permanent solution once we reach a safe location. I feel the others coming. It's now or never, Sarin."

After pulling Faith in for one last hug, Sarin padded over to the pantry entrance and had to hold back the full-on panic attack that threatened to take her over at the sight of her mother's dead body. Logically, Sarin knew her mom wasn't there anymore, but saying goodbye to her out loud felt like the right thing to do. "I'll love you forever, Mom. Until we meet again."

Sarin's heart broke into a thousand pieces as she left the only place she'd ever called home and slid into the passenger seat of Haven's car. She felt like she was falling down a rabbit hole, like the one in Alice in Wonderland. Only in this story, her wonderland was a hellscape.

"I understand how hard this is for you. I've had a lot of loss at the hands of monsters."

"What now?" Sarin asked, terrified to hear Haven's answer.

"Now, we go back to my rental house. I've been searching the forest for any signs of my mother's coven, but instead, I found you. It feels like it's meant to be."

This situation didn't feel like fate to Sarin, especially the part where she lost her mom and friend. "Since we're cousins, is your mother the witch they say burned her coven?"

Haven nodded as she put the car in reverse.

"Faith's mom told me my aunt turned against my grandmother, killing my father in the process."

Haven let out a long sigh. "My mother's story is complicated. The things the coven did to her were unspeakable, and she only started the fire to defend herself. I'm sorry about your father, and I hope he wasn't like the rest of the elders. It's a tragic story; when you're ready, I'll tell you the rest. That's why I'm here in Canada, Sarin. My mom disappeared when I was a child, and I need to know if she's still alive or if her coven did something to her."

Staring over at her cousin, Sarin was full of conflicting emotions. "You're the only family I have left now."

"Then, we're in this together."

"Wait. What about Faith's mother? Farrow's been searching the forest for some vortex. If we go there, won't she find us?"

"I can cloak us so she won't be able to sense our magic, and a simple glamour will hide your true face. If Faith's mom is looking for the vortex, she has an ulterior motive. The power in that place is dark. It deceives. It twisted our grandmother into a power-hungry monster and will do the same to anyone who tries to wield it.

Sarin shifted uncomfortably in the passenger as they drove through downtown. Passing by Mills, she wondered if she'd ever see her friends or Alex again. "All my instincts are telling me to trust you."

Smiling, Haven patted Sarin on the hand. "Once you awaken all that's inside you, you'll learn to master those instincts, my little spirit witch."

Sarin didn't know how she was supposed to feel. She'd always longed for this moment, this connection with someone from her father's side of her family. And with Haven, she could learn everything there was to know about magic. Still, the loss of her mother and Selene would forever haunt her. The feeling of finding and losing a part of herself simultaneously was overwhelming.

"I can help you process the trauma while I train you," Haven chimed in with the mind-reading shit again.

"Thank you," Sarin said because no other words felt right. "Together it is."

EPILOGUE

T HE DOPPELGÄNGER REFORMED NEAR a vast waterway, still wearing the visage of Sarin's mother. Until it killed another, it couldn't shapeshift. The blonde witch's spell had repelled it, but thanks to the pinch of Sarin's magic it still possessed, it managed to stop the magical tornado before it blew it into the ether. Annoyed by its temporary defeat, it stalked the shore, looking for a new body. It was late, and only a handful of people were milling around the lake. Soft music filled the air, and when it turned to see where it was coming from, it spotted a handsome man sitting alone on a park bench, strumming a guitar. It recognized him from Sarin's thoughts. Alex. Yes, his body would do just fine.

If it hadn't been so sloppy in its hasty disposal of Lynne's body, it could have kept up the ruse long enough to kill Sarin and absorb all of her savory magic. It was still learning, and mistakes had been made. But how convenient it was that it came upon another body the witch loved. The next time they met, things would be different. It would take it's time once it found Sarin, disguised as her past lover. And when it finally killed her, revenge for its confinement would be a sweet symphony of pain. Quietly approaching Alex from behind, it made quick work of snapping the boy's neck, and as his guitar crashed to the ground, it struck a melancholy chord that complimented the moment. The doppelgänger's bones popped and shifted as it grew taller and longer into its new form. This body felt strong. This body felt right. Dragging Alex's corpse to the nearby bridge, it threw what remained of the human into the muddy waters below. Satisfied with its choice, it walked down the bridge, whistling through its newfound lips.

The End

ABOUT THE AUTHOR

Angela Dunham is a Halloween-obsessed writer who loves to tell stories about all things that go bump in the night. Angela's writing spans genres focusing on young adult paranormal and dark fantasy with a sprinkle of horror. When Angela isn't writing, she can be found reading, wrangling her adorable son or drinking an iced chai tea latte.

Angela is the author of the Chronicles of the Fallon One Trilogy, several published Novella's, and The Delvaux Witches. Book One in The Delvaux Witches series will release in 2024.

For promotional material, release dates, and giveaways, follow her on social media.

Website: www.authorangeladunham.com

Instagram: @authorangeladunham

www.ingramcontent.com/pod-product-compliance
Lightning Source LLC
Chambersburg PA
CBHW050500110726
47899CB00003B/1012